MW01204710

CN
15.95

UGLY ANIMALS

Vultures

Kerri O'Donnell

PowerKiDS
press™

New York

Published in 2007 by The Rosen Publishing Group, Inc.
29 East 21st Street, New York, NY 10010

Book Design: Michael Ruberto

Photo Credits: Cover, p. 17 © Tony Campbell/Shutterstock; pp. 3, 7 © Ferenc Cegledi/Shutterstock; pp. 5, 19, 22 © Stefan Ekernas/Shutterstock; p. 9 © A. & E. Morris/VIREO; p. 11 © Dwight Lyman/Shutterstock; pp. 13, 15 © R. Day/VIREO; p. 21 © Paul S. Wolf/Shutterstock.

Library of Congress Cataloging-in-Publication Data

O'Donnell, Kerri, 1972-
  Vultures / Kerri O'Donnell.
     p. cm. - (Ugly animals)
  Includes bibliographical references and index.
  ISBN-13: 978-1-4042-3526-4
  ISBN-10: 1-4042-3526-4
  1. Vultures-Juvenile literature. I. Title.
  QL696.F32O36 2007
  598.9'2-dc22
                              2006014620

Manufactured in the United States of America

Contents

That Is One Ugly Bird!   4

Kinds of Vultures   6

A Gross Dinner   8

Vultures on a Diet?   10

Feeding the Baby   12

No Time for a Nest   14

Vulture Vacation   16

Birds on the Breeze   18

Vulture Against Vulture   20

Keeping It Clean   22

Glossary   23

Index   24

Web Sites   24

That Is One Ugly Bird!

Have you ever seen a vulture? Vultures are large birds of **prey**. This means they feed on other animals. You may have seen a vulture feeding on a dead animal by the side of the road. Gross!

Vultures usually have black, brown, or white feathers. They have bald heads and necks. They have hooked beaks for tearing apart food. Vultures may be ugly, but they have very good eyesight. This helps them find their food.

This is a black vulture. Look at its wrinkly head!

Kinds of Vultures

Vultures are found all over the world. The black vulture is the smallest and most common North American vulture. Turkey vultures are usually dark brown. They can have wings that are 6.5 feet (2 m) from tip to tip. Unlike most kinds of birds, turkey vultures have a good sense of smell. A vulture called the California **condor** is one of the largest kinds of vultures.

California condors have pink skin on their bald necks and heads.

A Gross Dinner

Vultures have a pretty gross diet—they eat dead animals! Vultures might eat a dead squirrel or deer on the side of the road. They might eat dead fish or a dead whale that has washed up on the beach. Vultures might even eat a dead elephant!

Vultures usually eat animals that have been dead for a while. As the dead animal rots, it begins to smell. The smell makes it easier for vultures to find it.

Turkey vultures often feed together on a dead animal.

Vultures on a Diet?

Vultures sometimes go a long time without food. If it can't find any dead animals to eat, a turkey vulture can live for several weeks without eating. A California condor can go even longer without food. When it finally finds a dead animal to munch on, it eats and eats. It eats so much that its **crop** bulges. A crop is a pouch where a vulture keeps its food before it goes to its stomach.

Turkey vultures use their sharp beaks to rip apart their food.

Feeding the Baby

We've learned that a vulture's diet is pretty gross. The way vultures feed their babies is gross, too. When vulture babies are small, their parents throw up partly **digested** meat for them to eat. When the babies get bigger, their parents cough up pieces of meat for them to eat.

Vultures throw up for other reasons, too. They throw up to make themselves lighter. This helps them fly away from their enemies more easily.

These baby vultures will eat meat their parents throw up for them!

No Time for a Nest

Many kinds of birds build nests to live in. Vultures don't waste time building nests. They find hidden places to lay their eggs. Then they lay their eggs right on the ground.

Vultures might lay their eggs in a fallen tree in the woods. They might lay eggs in a cave or in an empty building. Vultures are very careful when leaving or returning to their "nest." They don't want their enemies to see them.

Most female vultures lay between one and three eggs at a time.

Vulture Vacation

It's hard to eat your dinner when it's frozen. That's why many vultures **migrate** to warmer places during the winter. They go where they can find dead animals to eat that aren't too frozen to rip apart with their sharp beaks.

Many vultures that live in Canada or the northern United States migrate south during the winter. Some travel all the way to South America! There they hunt for food to eat.

Migrating turkey vultures travel together. These turkey vultures are resting on a branch.

Birds on the Breeze

Vultures try not to flap their wings too much when they fly. Instead, they use their large wings to **glide** through the air. This helps them save their **energy**. They search for warm air rising from the ground. The rising air carries the vultures upward. Then they glide downward until they find more warm air to carry them upward again. Vultures can also glide on winds that blow up the sides of mountains or hills.

They might be ugly up close, but vultures can look beautiful when gliding.

19

Vulture Against Vulture

Vultures are always looking for their next meal. They will follow other vultures to see what kind of food they have found. Turkey vultures find food with their great sense of smell. Black vultures can't smell well, but they have very good eyesight. They will fly high to look for turkey vultures. When they see a turkey vulture fly down toward the ground, they follow. The black vulture might then steal the turkey vulture's meal!

A black vulture will fight another vulture for a good meal.

Keeping It Clean

Vultures may be ugly, and their eating habits are really gross. However, vultures help us. They eat dead animals that have lots of nasty **germs** on them. If these germs get into streams and rivers, they can make animals and people sick. Vultures can eat these germs without getting sick. They are nature's cleaners!

Glossary

condor (KAHN-dohr) A kind of large vulture.

crop (KRAHP) A pouch inside the neck of many birds where food is stored.

digested (dy-JEHS-tuhd) When your body has broken down the food you eat.

energy (EH-nuhr-jee) The strength and ability to do things.

germ (JURM) A very tiny living thing that can cause sickness.

glide (GLYD) To fly smoothly and easily without moving the wings.

migrate (MY-grayt) To move from one place to another when the seasons change.

prey (PRAY) An animal that is hunted by another animal as food.

Index

B
babies, 12
bald, 4
beaks, 4, 16
birds of prey, 4
black vulture(s),
    6, 20

C
California condor,
    6, 10
crop, 10

E
eat(s), 8, 10, 12,
    16, 22
eggs, 14
enemies, 12, 14
eyesight, 4, 20

F
food, 4, 10, 16, 20

G
germs, 22
glide, 18

M
migrate, 16

S
smell, 6, 8, 20

T
throw up, 12
turkey vulture(s),
    6, 10, 20

W
wings, 6, 18

Web Sites

Due to the changing nature of Internet links, PowerKids Press has developed an online list of Web sites related to the subject of this book. This site is updated regularly. Please use this link to access the list: **http://www.powerkidslinks.com/uglyani/vultures/**